The Farmer and His Sons

Why should you work hard?

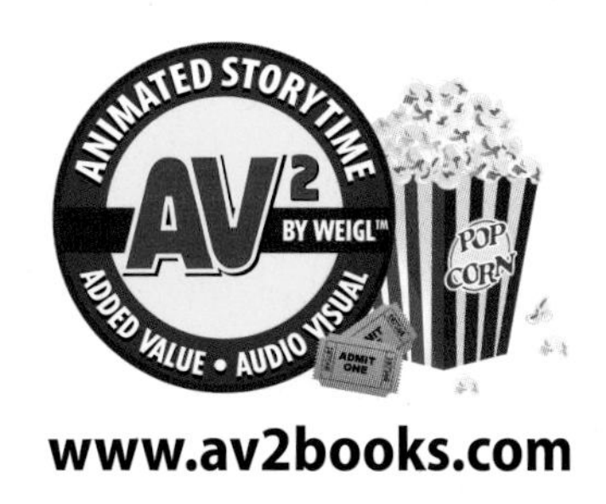

www.av2books.com

Go to www.av2books.com, and enter this book's unique code.

BOOK CODE

P51123

AV^2 by Weigl brings you media enhanced books that support active learning.

Published by AV^2 by Weigl
350 5th Avenue, 59th Floor New York, NY 10118

Library of Congress Cataloging-in-Publication Data
Fax 1-866-449-3445 for the attention of the Publishing Records department.

ISBN 978-1-62127-917-4 (Hardcover)
ISBN 978-1-48960-131-5 (Multi-user eBook)

Senior Editor: Heather Kissock
Project Coordinator: Alexis Roumanis
Art Director: Terry Paulhus

Printed in the United States in North Mankato, Minnesota
1 2 3 4 5 6 7 8 9 0 17 16 15 14 13

052013
WEP300513

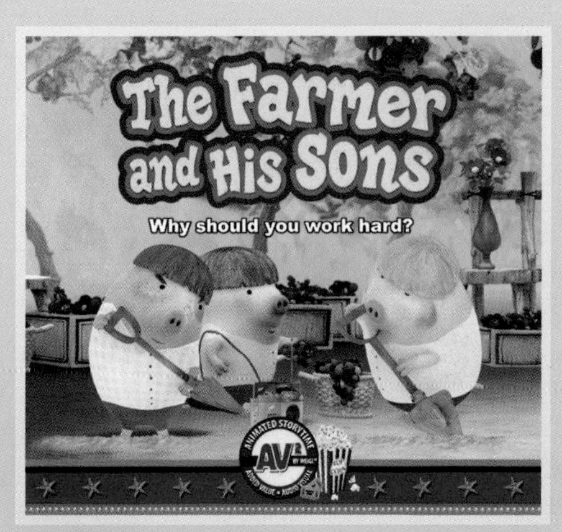

FABLE SYNOPSIS

For thousands of years, parents and teachers have used memorable stories called fables to teach simple moral lessons to children.

In the Aesop's Fables by AV^2 series, classic fables are given a lighthearted twist. These familiar tales are performed by a troupe of animal players whose endearing personalities bring the stories to life.

In *The Farmer and His Sons*, Aesop and his troupe teach their audience about the value of a hard day's work. They learn that hard work is its own reward.

This AV^2 media enhanced book comes alive with...

Animated Video
Watch a custom animated movie.

Try This!
Complete activities and hands-on experiments.

Key Words
Study vocabulary, and complete a matching word activity.

Quiz
Test your knowledge.

Why should you work hard?

AV^2 Storytime Navigation

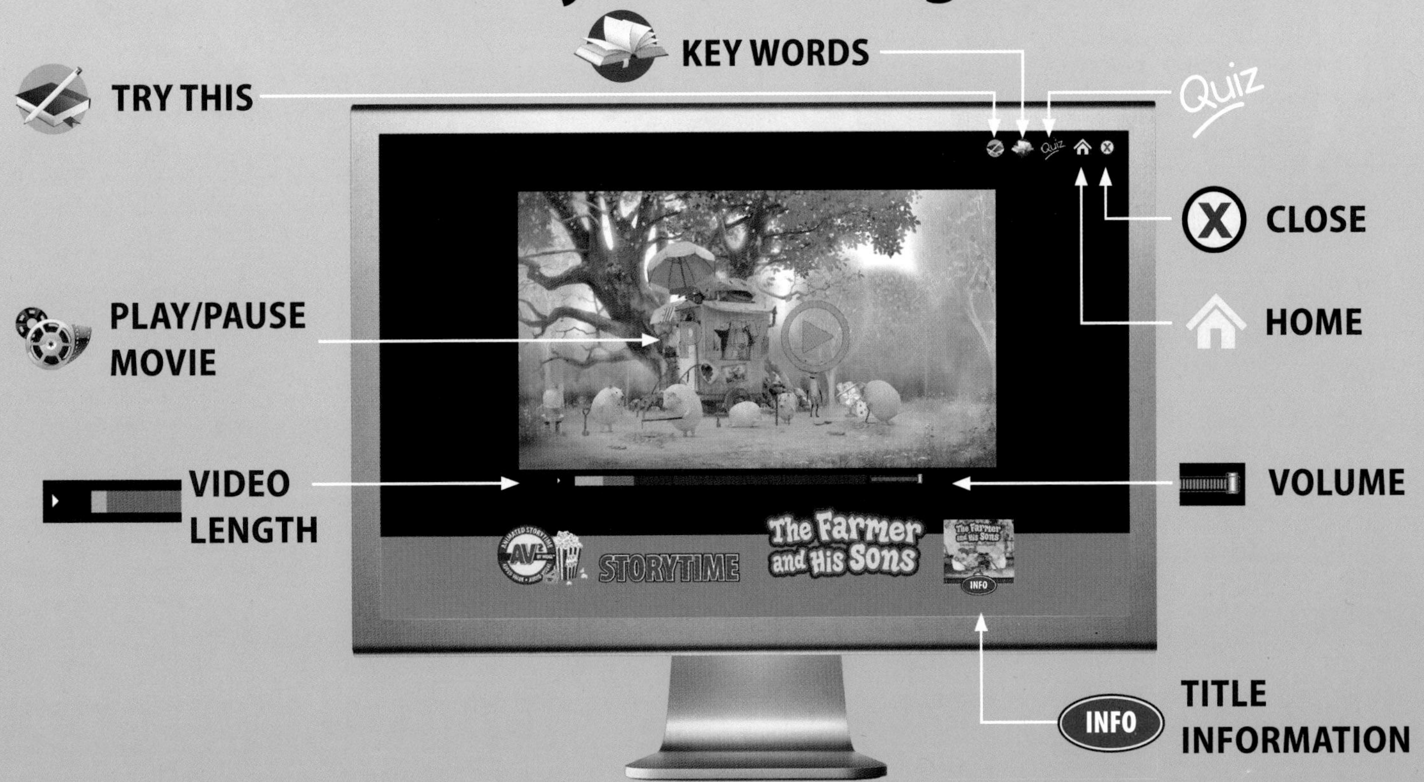

The Players

The Players

Aesop
I am the leader of Aesop's Theater, a screenwriter, and an actor.
I can be hot-tempered, but I am also soft and warm-hearted.
Libbit
I am an actor and a prop man.
I think I should have been a lion, but I was born a rabbit.
Presy
I am the manager of Aesop's Theater.
I am also the narrator of the plays.

Elvis
I like dance and music. I am artistic. I am very good at drawing.
Bogart
I am the strongest and the oldest pig. I always do whatever I want.
Audrey
I am a very good and caring pig. If someone cries, I cry with them. I never lie.
Milala
I think I am cute. I like to get attention from the other animals.
Goddard
I am very greedy. I like food.

The Story

Aesop and his acting troupe were telling everyone about their new play.

The Shorties were making a lot of noise.

"We'll present *The Farmer and His Sons* tonight. Please join us!" yelled out Aesop.

Aesop heard a loud crash in the forest.

A big bear ran out of the bushes.

The bear was very upset.

Aesop and the Shorties dropped their costumes.

The bear chased them through the forest.

The bear finally grew tired.

"You woke me from my winter sleep!" growled the bear.

"I'm sorry," said Aesop. "We did not see you sleeping.

Let us make it up to you. Come watch our play tonight."

That night, the bear and all of the animals came out to watch the new play.

A hard-working farmer fell sick. He called his three sons to his side to give them his parting words.

"My sons, I have something to tell you."

The three sons listened closely.

"When you were all very young, I hid a treasure in the grape farm. You will all live comfortably when you find it."

Soon after, the farmer passed away.

The morning after the farmer's death, the three sons went to the grape farm.

They worked hard to find the treasure, but they could not see it.

A few months passed. There was still no sign of the treasure.

Summer came, and it was time to harvest their crops.

The three sons had a rich harvest of grapes.

Now they understood their father's last request.

Hard work was the real treasure, and they had found it together.

When the play had ended, everyone gathered together.

"Good job! Let's do this play tomorrow," said Aesop.

"The bear wants to see the same play tomorrow."

"Are you sure we can?" asked Libbit.

"What do you mean?" asked Aesop.

"The Shorties ate all the grapes!" said Libbit.

Aesop looked over and noticed the Shorties were just finishing the last of the grapes.

"No! The grapes are for the performance. I have no money to buy more!" cried Aesop.

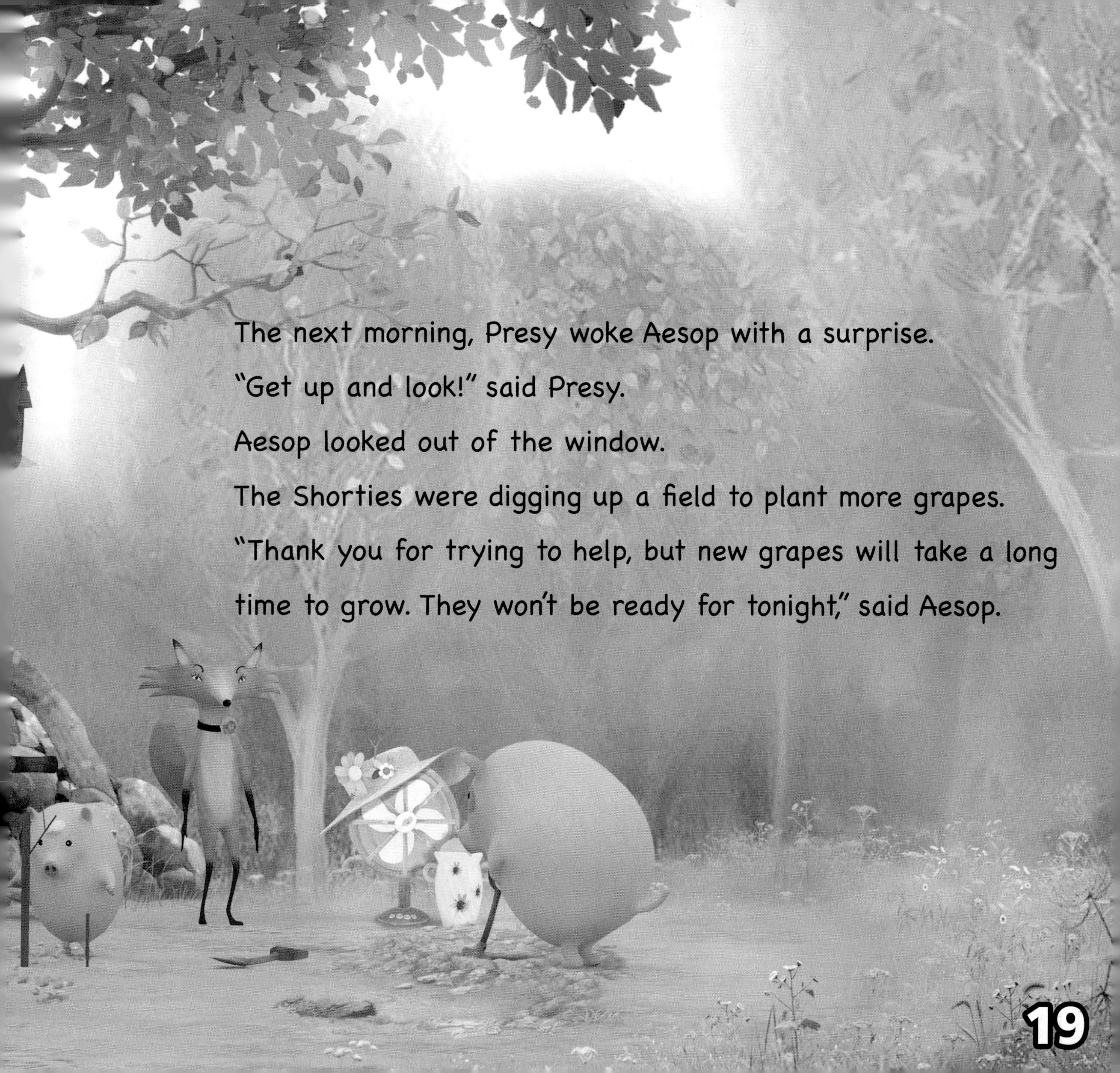

The next morning, Presy woke Aesop with a surprise.

"Get up and look!" said Presy.

Aesop looked out of the window.

The Shorties were digging up a field to plant more grapes.

"Thank you for trying to help, but new grapes will take a long time to grow. They won't be ready for tonight," said Aesop.

A raccoon saw that the soil had been dug up.
He came to speak to Aesop.
"Were you digging here?" asked
the raccoon.
Aesop was nervous that the
Shorties had dug up the
raccoon's field.
"Yes. The Shorties were
trying to help me," Aesop
said with a big sigh.
Presy and Aesop thought that
the Shorties were in trouble.

The raccoon looked at the ground. "They dug very well. Now it is good for farming. Do you think you could sell me this land so I can start a farm?"

"This is not our land," said Presy.

"Really! Then I can plant seeds here?" said the raccoon.

"You have to pay the Shorties for their work. They dug it up!" said Libbit.

The raccoon gave Libbit some money.

Libbit and Aesop bought more grapes with the money.
They put the baskets in front of the Shorties.
"Hard work can be rewarding," said Aesop.
"Now we can perform the play tonight," said Libbit.

The Shorties were excited by the reward. They asked Aesop if they could keep digging rather than perform.
"We need your help to make the play a success. You have to act in the play!" said Aesop.

The Shorties looked sad when Aesop told them they could no longer dig.

Aesop thought for a moment.

"Okay. You can dig during the day and perform at night. The money you raise from digging can help pay for our theater."

The Shorties were excited to hear that their hard work would benefit their friends.

Hard work is its own reward.

What Is a Story?

Players

Who is the story about? The characters, or players, are the people, animals, or objects that perform the story. Characters have personality traits that contribute to the story. Readers understand how a character fits into the story by what the character says and does, what others say about the character, and how others treat the character.

Setting

Where and when do the events take place? The setting of a story helps readers visualize where and when the story is taking place. These details help to suggest the mood or atmosphere of the story. A setting is usually presented briefly, but it explains whether the story is taking place in the past, present, or future and in a large or small area.

Plot

What happens in the story? The plot is a story's plan of action. Most plots follow a pattern. They begin with an introduction and progress to the rising action of events. The events lead to a climax, which is the most exciting moment in the story. The resolution is the falling action of events. This section ties up loose ends so that readers are not left with unanswered questions. The story ends with a conclusion that brings the events to a close.

Point of View

Who is telling the story? The story is normally told from the point of view of the narrator, or storyteller. The narrator can be a main character or a less important character in the story. He or she can also be someone who is not in the story but is observing the action. This observer may be impartial or someone who knows the thoughts and feelings of the characters. A story can also be told from different points of view.

Dialogue

What type of conversation occurs in the story? Conversation, or dialogue, helps to show what is happening. It also gives information about the characters. The reader can discover what kinds of people they are by the words they say and how they say them. Writers use dialogue to make stories more interesting. In dialogue, writers imitate the way real people speak, so it is written differently than the rest of the story.

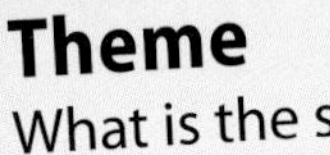

Theme

What is the story's underlying meaning? The theme of a story is the topic, idea, or position that the story presents. It is often a general statement about life. Sometimes, the theme is stated clearly. Other times, it is suggested through hints.

The Farmer and His Sons Quiz

1
Where did the farmer say the treasure was buried?

2
What did the Shorties eat?

3
What were the Shorties doing when Aesop woke up?

4
Who paid the Shorties for their work in the field?

5
What did Aesop and Libbit do with the money?

6
What did the players learn?

Answers:
1. The grape farm
2. The grapes
3. Digging up the field
4. The raccoon
5. Bought more grapes
6. Hard work will pay off in the end.

Key Words

Research has shown that as much as 65 percent of all written material published in English is made up of 300 words. These 300 words cannot be taught using pictures or learned by sounding them out. They must be recognized by sight. This book contains 134 common sight words to help young readers improve their reading fluency and comprehension. This book also teaches young readers several important content words, such as proper nouns. These words are paired with pictures to aid in learning and improve understanding.

Page	Sight Words First Appearance
4	a, also, am, an, and, be, been, but, can, have, I, man, of, plays, should, the, think, was
5	always, animals, at, do, food, from, get, good, if, like, never, other, them, to, very, want, with
6	about, his, new, out, story, their, us, were
9	big, in, through
11	all, came, come, did, it, let, make, me, my, night, not, our, said, see, that, up, watch, we, you
13	after, away, farm, find, give, hard, he, live, side, something, soon, tell, three, when, will, words, young
14	could, few, found, had, last, no, now, still, there, they, time, together, went, work
16	are, asked, for, just, mean, more, over, same, this, what
19	grow, help, long, look, next, plant, take
20	here, saw, thought
23	is, land, really, so, some, then, well
24	by, keep, need, put, than, your
27	day, end, hear, off, would

Page	Content Words First Appearance
4	actor, leader, lion, manager, narrator, rabbit, screenwriter, theater
5	attention, dance, music, pig
6	farmer, noise, sons, tonight, troupe
9	bear, bushes, costumes, forest
11	sleep
13	treasure
14	crops, harvest, summer
16	grapes, money
19	field, morning, surprise, window
20	raccoon, sigh, soil
23	ground, seeds
24	baskets, reward
27	friends

Check out av2books.com for your animated storytime media enhanced book!

1. Go to av2books.com
2. Enter book code **P51123**
3. Fuel your imagination online!

www.av2books.com

AV² Storytime Navigation

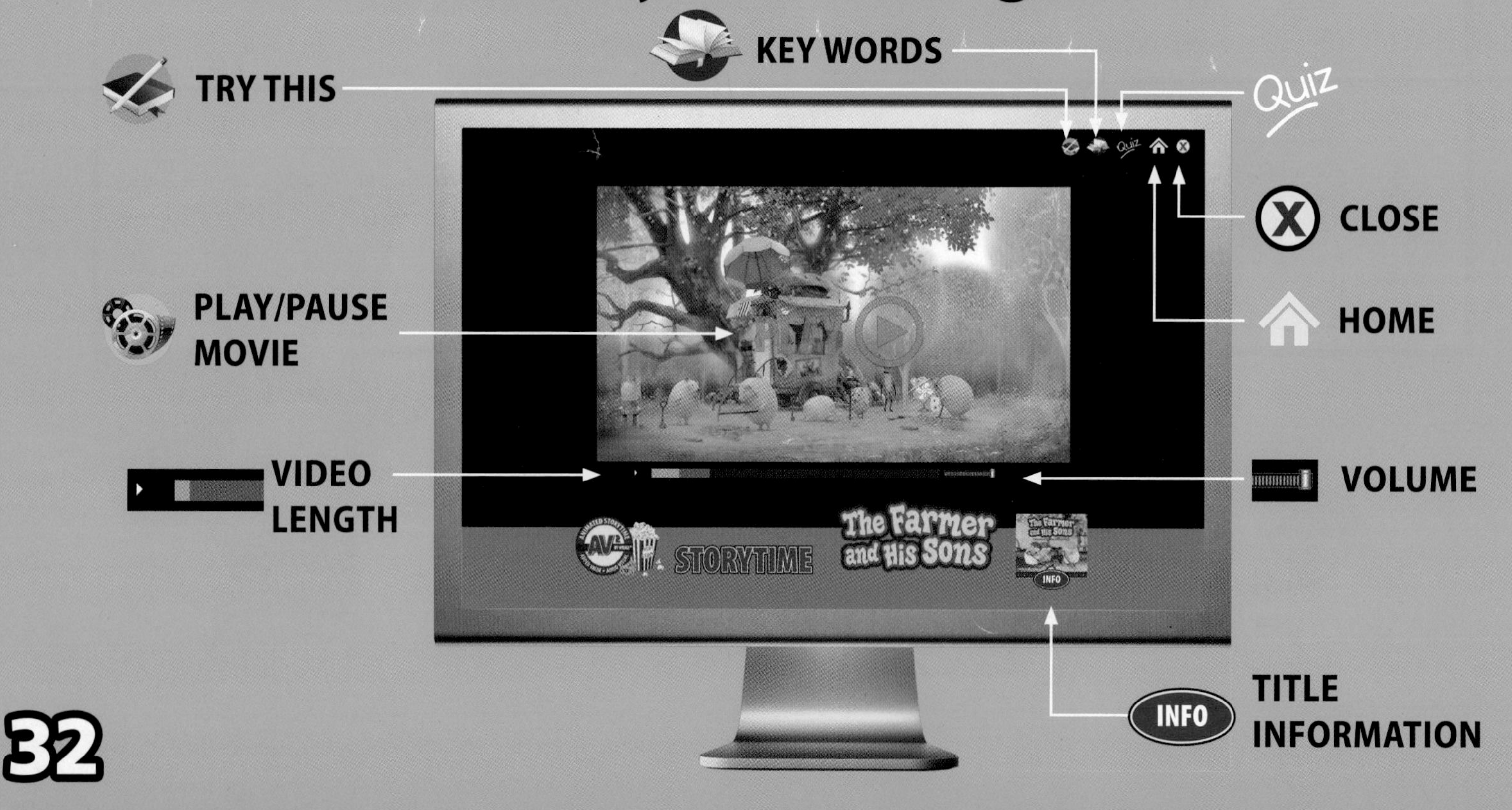